Nemanee

Written & Illustrated by Kelsey C Roy

For Nola -

For all the laughter, love and light
that made bright days of long, late nights.

There was a town named Nemanee,
a small, quaint, quiet place.
It slept on hillsides by the sea
in a quite forgotten space.
And in the center of this town
there was a boring street,
with boring homes of boring brown,
spaced out by boring feet.
Nothing ever happened here,
and nothing seemed to change,
until one day one wish made clear
that all would soon be strange.

In the third house on the right
there lived a pair of twins.
The two of them were very bright
and matched from outside, in.
In fact they were so very close
in eyes, nose, hair and heart
that only Dad and Momma both
could tell the two apart.

He looked like him and him like he.
They'd nothing not the same,
but sameness gave them unity
which made them hard to name.

Jacob, Jake, Jimmy or Jason or John?
Tom, Michael, Bill, Billy, Alexander or Don?
Marty, Matt, Martin, Chase, Timothy, George?
Frank, Henry, Ben, Brently or Paul III and IV?
It wasn't till then that the right names just hit,
as if by some magical way.
Patty and Paul named them Parker and Pip,
so Pip and Parker Piepepper they'd stay.

Never before had the neighborhood known
such disasters before these two boys.
There were action men standing where flowers had grown
and the yard was all littered with toys.

Squirrels would scurry and rabbits would run.
Birds would all flee to their trees.
Whenever it saw the Piepepper twins come,
Nature was never at ease.

Together they seemed to make rigid worlds bend
while their games would start blurring the lines,
erasing the wall between real and pretend
with imaginations combined.

When it got dark and before their goodnights,
the boys had a bubble bath battle,
with bubble block bricks and bubble ball fights
fought from two bubble-built castles.

Then one night their father said,
"You two are like fish from the sea!
You're soaked from all ten toes to head,
and look! There's a scale on your knee!"

"No there's not!" Pip laughed aloud,
"Boys can't turn to fish!"

But then their father raised a brow,
"Well maybe they could if you wish."

"Can we really turn from boys to fish?"
Pip asked as he crawled into bed.

"Can we really have scales and tails that swish
and breathe underwater instead?"

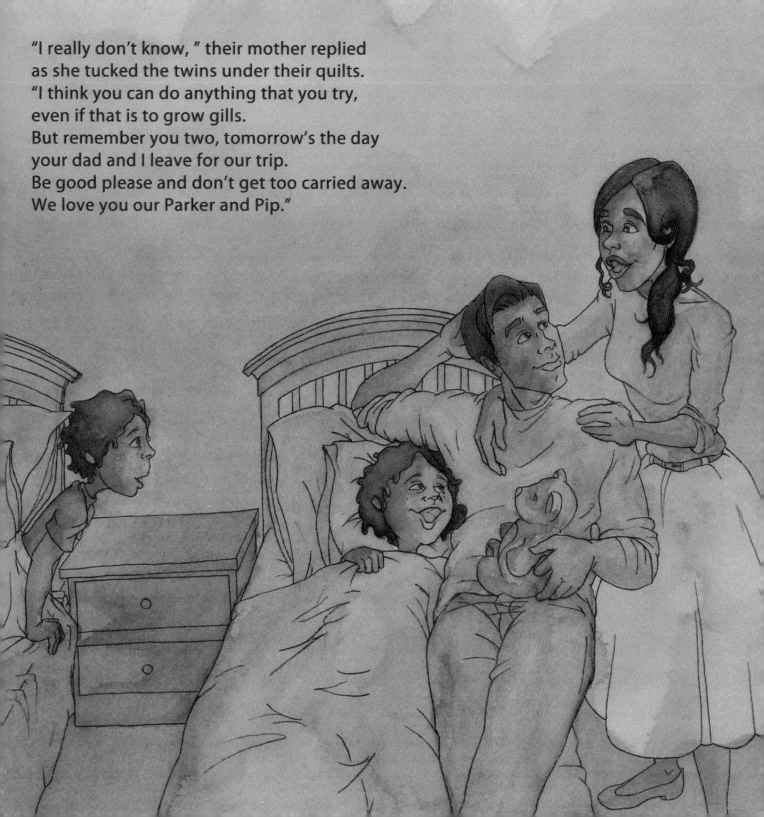

"I really don't know, " their mother replied
as she tucked the twins under their quilts.
"I think you can do anything that you try,
even if that is to grow gills.
But remember you two, tomorrow's the day
your dad and I leave for our trip.
Be good please and don't get too carried away.
We love you our Parker and Pip."

The next morning the boys woke in surprise
to find an odd, shining glass sphere.
Inside swam a fish with wild, wide eyes
and flowing, long fins, very sheer.

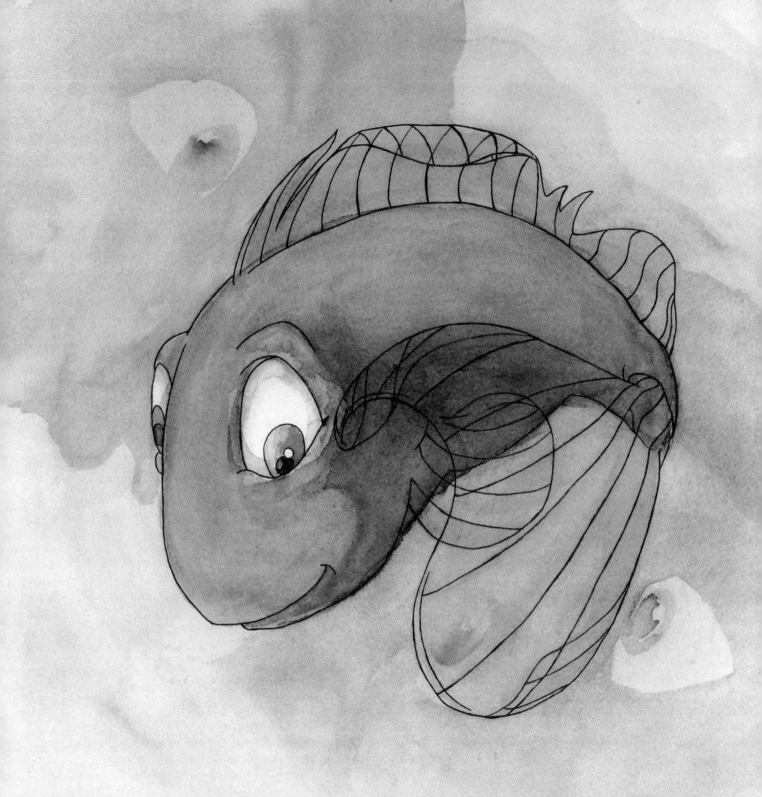

"They left it for you," shot a voice like a dart,
"for company while they are gone."
The voice came from a face that was sour and tart
and looked like it needed to yawn.

Her name was Ms. Sampson. She lived right next door.
The boys didn't care for her much.
They called her Surly Ma'am Sampson, the batty old bore,
who walked like a cranky old duck.
She hated most children, this much they knew,
but her reasons were rather unclear.
The smaller they were, the meaner she grew,
and the more severe was her sneer.

"Don't expect me to play in your games
or to laugh at your fanciful tales.
I will not tolerate you making up names,
nor will I listen to your screaming or wails.
I do not like pouting so don't even begin.
And I won't give you candy or sweets.
Sugar makes monsters of naughty children
and it also rots out all your teeth.
I think play should be quiet if not all the way silent,
and bedtimes are strictly enforced.
I think watching TV makes kids grow up violent,
and that includes music of course."

After a breakfast of sprout-omelets and pears
the twins ran back up to their room.
They played all day hidden safely upstairs,
away from their sitter of doom.

The poor fish watched the Piepeppers pretend,
all alone and unable to play.
"It must be so lonely not having a friend,"
Pip paused their game to say.

"I know!" said Parker, "We'll make a wish!
We'll wish and we'll set him free.
Then you and I both can be friends with our fish,
I, him, he, you and you, me."

So wish they did, those powerful twins
though they were not aware
of what consequences would begin
once they wished for a fish to breathe air!

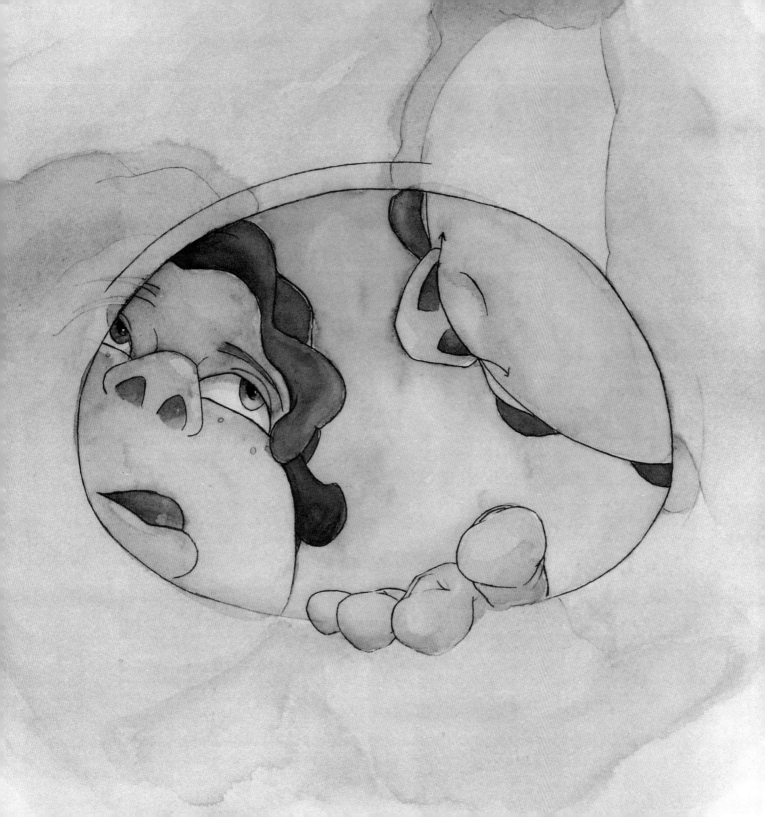

First a loud POW and a CRACKLE and POP
came from the glistening bowl.
Then sparkling white light poured from the top,
filling the room with false snow.

The boys didn't budge or alter their gaze.
All they could do was stare,
because there without water, above all the haze,
swam their fish in nothing but air!
It gave a quick swish of its shimmering tail
then darted around the room.
The boys jumped up to follow its trail,
and they danced in the light of the moon.

Then just before sleep washed over all three,
Parker ventured to say,
"Why don't we wish for some fish from the sea
to come to our house to play?"
They made this wish once, then two times for luck,
but no bright light filled the room.
Their eyes shut so tight they were sure to get stuck
yet still not magic ensued.

"I guess it's not working," pouted poor Pip
as he reached to turn out the light.

Then softly into slumber they slipped,
but the sea was not sleepy that night.

At breakfast the twins slumped into their chairs,
then quickly shot back from their plates.
On top seemed to be gray oatmeal with hairs,
sure to bring them to their fates.
But before Ms. Ma'am Sampson could force them to eat
what she called her "breakfast delight",
a very loud WHOMP shook the house and their feet,
and Ma'am Sampson screamed out in great fright.

The three of them rushed out into the street
to see if that noise was a spoof,
but there big enough for the neighbors to see
sat a squid on top of the roof!

"Oh my heavens!" Ms. Sampson cried out
and nearly fainted away.
"How could this even come about?
What will the neighbors say?"

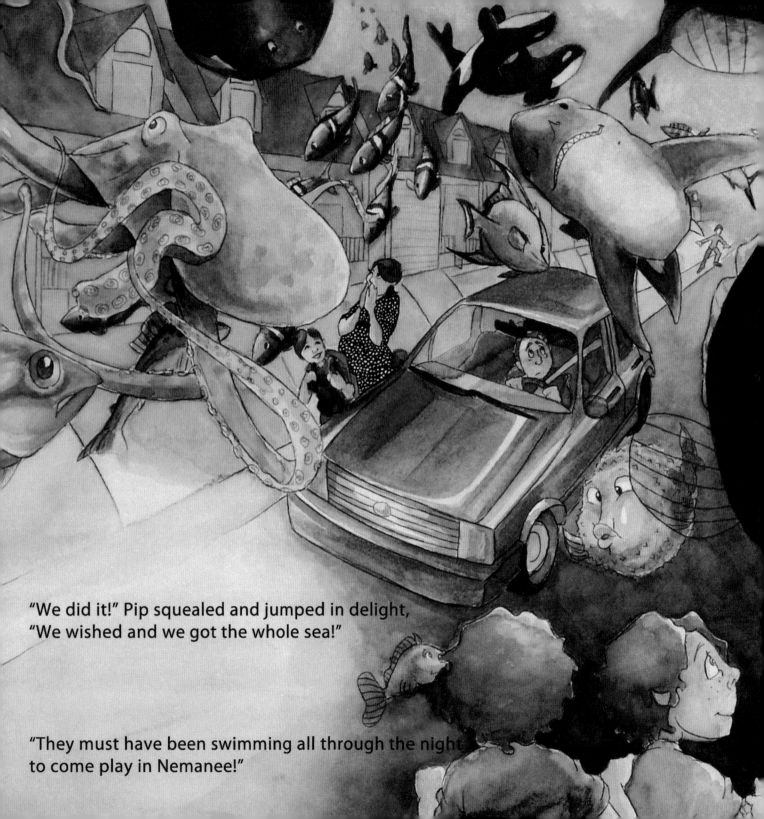

"We did it!" Pip squealed and jumped in delight,
"We wished and we got the whole sea!"

"They must have been swimming all through the night
to come play in Nemanee!"

"You did this?!" Ms. Sampson shrieked in dismay,
"You brought all these beastly things here?"

"Mom says we sometimes get carried away,"
said Parker with eyes full of cheer.

The street was a bustle and everyone knew
the Piepepper twins must be the cause.
So when news vans arrived and asked, "How?" and "Who?"
the neighbors placed blame without pause.
Camera men wriggled and raced down the road
trying to be first on the scene.
People from all over, both young and quite old
were racing to Nemanee.

"Are you the boys who did all this?"
asked Chip Chase from News of Nee.

"Can you tell us how you got these fish
to fly here from the sea?"
"We made a wish," Pip simply said.
Then Parker added in,
"You see, our fish needed a friend,
so these are all for him."

The whole world watched in disbelief
as countries all around
reported sea life leaving reefs
and hovering over ground.

By nightfall nearly every fish
from every ocean far
had found its way to grant their wish
and swim up with the stars.
In fact so many fish had come
to swim above the town,
the sky was rather overrun
and none could move around!

Panicked parents and uncles and aunts,
doctors of science and oceans and plants,
nervous and flustered neighbors galore,
all of them rushed to the Piepepper door.

"Please put them back!" one pleaded in fright
as another cried out, "This just isn't right!"

"Fish don't belong in the air above homes,"
said Dr. Dan Dowdy in dreary, dull drones.

"The oceans will sink! The tides will give way!"
"And what about ships? They'll all go astray!"
"And what of our kids?" cried Ms. Fushia Flatts,
"What of our dogs and our birds and our cats?"

On they all bumbled and blustered and begged
until their faces were blue.
Finally it was Parker Piepepper who said,
"I know what we have to do."

With that the twins held tight their hands
and asked with all their might
for the fish to fly back over sands
and return their gift of flight.

They watched through wet, sad, sodden eyes
till skies again were clear.
Even Ma'am Sampson waved goodbye
and dried a single tear.

"I'm rather proud of you," she said
"for doing what was best."
She patted each one on the head,
"Though I still think you're pests."

They will not know how it came to be
that they later woke up in their room.
They won't be sure if it was all a dream
or if it had all been true.
But they'll hear soft laughter in the hall
and to sweet slumber drift.
Those twins will want for nothing at all
as they sleep tight next to their fish.